A Splash of Sass

SASSAFRAS GETS A PUPPY

A Splash of Sass

SASSAFRAS GETS A PUPPY

Written by Janet R. Adams

Illustrated by Aleksander Jasinski

Published by Chasing Fireflies Publishing LLC

Oklahoma City, Oklahoma

First published 2021

Written by Janet R. Adams

Edited by Lisa Davis

Illustrated by Aleksander Jasinski

Publishing and Design Services: MelindaMartin.me

Library of Congress Control Number: 2021901049

ISBN (paperback): 978-1-953499-03-5

ISBN (hardback): 978-1-953499-05-9

ISBN (e-book): 978-1-953499-04-2

This book is dedicated to my

husband, my biggest supporter.

Thank you for believing in me.

—Janet

Chapter 1

"SASSAFRAS!" MOM CALLED FROM THE HALLWAY.

I sat up after hearing her shout. My room was supposed to be cleaned last night, but I was way too busy reading my *All About Dogs* library book. It was like it was made especially for me.

I ran like lightning from the living room. When I got to the hallway, I saw Mom. She looked madder than an old, wet hen. (I happen to know what those mad wet hens look like. I may have accidentally knocked one into the pool at my grandma's house last summer.)

I hugged the wall tightly and tip-toed just out of Mom's view. Once I got into the laundry room, I quietly crawled up the laundry chute that goes right to my room. It was like climbing the slide at preschool: Easy peasy lemon squeezy!

I flung toys over my shoulder, left and right. I grabbed books and slid across the slick floor with my fuzzy socks. I slid myself right over to my bookshelf like an ice skating princess. I spotted some of my favorite stuffies across the room and took off running. That's when it happened! I stepped on a block. The pain ran from my toes up to my nose.

I almost let out a shriek but caught my mouth with my hand just in time! This had not gone as planned. I hopped on one foot for a while before deciding to crawl. I crawled over to Georgie, my stuffed monkey. I threw him on top of my bed. Thankfully, my bed was already made. I slept on top of my quilt so that I wouldn't need to make it today. I was getting really good at figuring out shortcuts.

"Sass! Where are you? Your room looks like a tornado hit it!" Mom hollered from the hallway, not realizing I had snuck past her.

I took a quick glance around my room and spotted my unicorn pajamas hanging on my lamp. I hobbled over to them and then darted for the laundry chute. I slid face-first right onto the laundry room floor, and my pajamas landed on top of my head. As I pulled them off my head, I saw Mom's shoes just a few inches away. They were tapping. Really, really tapping.

"Oh! Hi, Mom." I shot up from the floor and giggled nervously.

"Sassafras, what are you doing?" That was what my parents used to call me when I was a sassy toddler. My real name was Avril. The nickname stuck to me like glue. Many people just called me "Sass."

"Who? Me?"

"Yes, you," Mom said while giving me THE look. You know THE look. The one that your mom gives you when you are about to get THE talkin' to.

"Well, it's a funny story." I looked around and wondered what kind of story I might tell her that would be funny enough to get myself out of this pickle.

"Sass, we've talked about this. You HAVE to keep your room clean if you want a dog. How can you take care of a dog if you can't keep your room clean?"

"I'll do better, Momma. I promise." I gave her my sweetest smile.

Mom ruffled my hair. "Now, go get your lunch bag and backpack. You're going to be late for the bus. Your brother and I will meet you at the bus stop after school."

I grabbed my things before running out the door and down the sidewalk to the bus stop. I did not want to miss the bus!

Chapter 2

By the time I had gotten to the bus stop, I was out of breath. I could already see the bus coming down the road. “Close one!” I said, wiping my short brown hair out of my face.

“Hey there, Sass! Have you gotten your puppy yet?” Chloe asked eagerly, just like she has every day for the past month.

Chloe was my bestie-above-the-restie. My B-F-F. My super favoritist person in the whole-wide neighborhood.

“Not yet. Dad said it might be soon, but I have to keep my room clean and help out my mom around the house.”

“I’m so excited for a widdle puppy baby!” Chloe

squealed as the bus came rumbling up the street. "I have always wanted a puppy. Every Christmas, I ask for a puppy, and do you know what I get?"

I shook my head "no" like I had not heard this story fifteen times before.

"I get a toy puppy!"

"This year will be your year, Chloe. I can just feel it!" I said hopefully.

The bus came to a stop, and we hopped up the steps and then ran to the back of the bus. That was where the cool kids liked to sit and compare lunch boxes. But Chloe and I liked to sit there until they got on the bus and made us move.

We sat down, and I got out my library book and started flipping through the pages. "Look here! I love this one. It reminds me of Lady from *Lady and the Tramp!"*

"Ohhhh. What is it?" Chloe asked.

"A cockla-span-yell."

"Is that really how you say it?"

"Well, look here. Read it for yourself."

The bus windows were down, so Chloe had me hold her hair back so she could read my book. "Yep. That's definitely a cockla-span-yell."

"My super-favoritist is a golden retreeber," I said, pointing at a picture.

The boy in the seat in front of us got interested in our conversation suddenly. "It's 'cocker spaniel' and 'golden retriever,' you know," he said with a shaking head.

"That's what I said, silly goose!" I said with a shaking head to match his shaking head.

Chloe ignored the boy. "Well, did you decide? A boy dog or a girl dog?"

"I think I want a girl. Then I can put some razzle-dazzle pink nail polish on her little princess paws. Mom got me some really cool glittery nail polish too."

Chloe's eyes got big. She was as excited as I was. "What about her name?" she asked.

"Oh, I don't know. I like Cleo. Mom said I should name her Sunny, and Dad thinks I should name her

Princess. And my silly brother says I should name her Butter." I shook my head and laughed. "What do you think?"

Chloe got to thinking up a storm. She finally exclaimed, "Goldie!"

Man! That was a good thinking storm she had. I loved it! That's why she was my bestie-above-the-restie! Goldie was the perfect name.

I pushed my glasses back up on my nose and pulled out my favorite blue and green sloth pencil and my bright pink journal. The bus bumped me real good as it rolled to a stop at the next bus stop, but I got "G O L D I E" written in big letters. Next, I drew a picture of a golden retriever with a big bow on her head.

Chloe leaned over and said, "Wow. That's a great picture. It's beautiful!"

"Thanks, Chloe!" I closed my journal and stuffed it and the pencil back into my backpack.

GOLDIE
All about DOGS

Just then, the cool kids that like the backseat got on the bus. They pointed at Chloe and me and told us to get out of their seats. Chloe and I moved up to the middle row of the bus. That was where the very coolest kids really liked to sit. (That's us, in case you didn't know!) We spent the rest of the ride to school telling each other jokes like, "What do you call someone who takes a frog's picture? A frogtographer!" Get it?!

Pretty soon, we arrived at school. Chloe and I had been in the same class together two years in a row. It only took the teacher one week to realize we probably should not sit next to each other. We got the giggles a lot!

We settled into our seats and started our day writing in our journals. Our journals had a big space to draw pictures. Under your picture, you were supposed to write a story.

"Today, we are going to write a story about something you really want," Mrs. Brown said. "For example, it could be a toy or food that you really wish you had. Write in your journal what you want and why you want it. Then, draw a special picture and color it in with your crayons."

This was a no-brainer. I knew exactly what I was going to be writing about in my journal! I drew Goldie just like I had on the bus. I made her yellow with a big pink bow on her head. I made her eyes blue, just like mine.

Beneath the picture, I wrote, "I want a puppy. I will name her Goldie. I want a puppy so that I will always have a good friend to play with any time I want. I can take care of her and be her mommy."

I shut my school journal and hugged it tightly. I hoped that someday soon I would have my very own real-life puppy.

Chapter 3

THE REST OF THE SCHOOL DAY WENT GREAT! I sat by Chloe and Sophie at lunch. Sophie is my other BFF. Chloe, Sophie, and I played together at recess. Like every day, I climbed to the tippy-top of the monkey bars. My legs love to climb, and the monkey bars are the best place to climb on our playground. And that afternoon, our teacher gave the whole class lollipops for being so good all day. It had been the best day!

After school was over, Chloe and I rode the bus home. Usually, Chloe would come to my house after school, but I had to help Mom with chores so I could get a puppy. It's so boring doing chores!

When we made it to our bus stop, I hippity-hopped right off the bus and started to run home. Then I heard, "Ah-eeeee!" That's how my little brother says, "Sassy." Little brothers like to do that—say things all cute. I twirled around to see Mom and Asher waiting for me on the nearby bench. I waved real big and skipped over to them. Chloe skipped along right behind me.

Asher hopped down from the bench and ran toward me. He threw his little arms around me as far as they'd go.

"Aw! Hey buddy. What's my baby brudder doing?"

"Ah-ee! We get puppies today!"

I felt my eyes grow so big that I thought they might take over my whole face. I looked at Mom to see if this was really real. And do you know what?! She smiled big and nodded her head YES! I could not believe it! We were going to get puppies! Wait.

"Puppies? As in . . . more than one puppy?" I asked.

Mom nodded her head again. I must have fallen

off the bus and hit my head. This really was the best day ever. Best. Day. Ever!

Chloe and I both squealed and jumped up and down!

"I thought that a puppy might need a friend to play with, so you and Asher can both pick one out," Mom said.

I wrapped Mom up in a hug so tight that I bet she thought I was going to squeeze her to pieces. I could have shot to the moon. I was so excited!

Mom smiled. "Aside from this morning, you have done a great job keeping your room clean and helping with chores, so your dad and I agreed you can get a puppy."

Chloe squealed again. "I can't wait to meet her! Can I meet her today? Please!"

I squealed too. "Pleeeeeeasseee!"

"Yes. Chloe, I will call your mom when we get back. We'll see you very soon." Mom looked at me and said, "Come on, Sass. I parked just around the corner. We have to be there by 4 o'clock to meet the puppies. That's three Georges from now!" We all ran to the car and got buckled in.

Mom told us time in Georges because Asher still didn't know how to tell time. An episode of *Curious George* on TV was about 10 minutes long. Three Georges was only 30 minutes, but this was the longest three Georges ever. It felt like we had driven for hours. You know time stops when you are excited.

I decided to pass the time by drawing in my pink journal. I couldn't wait to meet Goldie. I used my crayons to make her fur yellow and her bow pink, just like I had in my school journal. But then I realized that I didn't know what kind of puppies we are going to get.

"Mom, I was so excited that I forgot to ask. What kind of puppies are we getting?"

"Guess," Mom said.

And would you know that I guessed right the first try! We were going to get golden retriever puppies!

Soon after that, Asher started getting hangry. You know, when you are hungry and angry? That's called hangry. And boy, was he ever. He wouldn't stop talking about it. "My belly rubbing, Momma! I wanna go to chick-fa-way and get a shamwich! It's my fravorite." It was a good thing that he was so cute because he seriously didn't know how to speak English.

Then, Mom spied him from the rear-view mirror. He was picking his boogers. "Asher, stop picking your nose."

With a big sigh and frown, he said, "Mom, I'm not! I'm putting them back in!"

Needless to say, this was a really long car ride with Mr. Hangry. I went back to drawing in my journal. I added a dog house, grass, trees, the sun, and a rainbow to the picture of Goldie.

A moment later, we started heading down some winding dirt roads and finally pulled into an old farmhouse. There was a tire swing, a great big red barn, some horses and cows out in their pasture, and a dog on their front porch. It looked like a good place for puppies to live, but my house would be a great place. You know, since I live there and stuff.

I tried to get out of my car seat, but I got all tangled up and half-fell out of the car when Mom opened the door. I was only a couple of inches away from eating the dirt when a big golden retriever came over and started licking my face. I got up in a hurry, afraid she was going to lick my freckles off and eat my glasses! Behind her came one, two, three, four, five, six, SEVEN puppies. They were like little golden fuzzy chunks that wagged their tails so hard their whole bodies wagged too! Some of them had pink collars, and others had blue collars.

Asher ran around the car and was immediately tackled to the ground. "I being licked to death, Ah-ee!" he screamed. I wasn't sure if he was terrified or just excited. It turned out that Asher really enjoyed being licked to death. "They squishing my tummy!" he called out while one of the puppies jumped on top of his belly.

“Look at you, giggle guts,” Mom said. “You found some friends.”

One of the little puppies with a blue collar stopped licking Asher long enough to scratch his own face with his paw, and then he fell right over. Another puppy with a pink collar started sassing him for being a klutz. I knew then and there that I had found Goldie. She was a little sassy, just like me! I did a big pat on my legs. The sassy puppy ran over, along with all six of her brothers and sisters. I laid down and let them pounce on me.

“Best day ever!” I shouted from underneath the pile of puppies.

A lady came over to meet us. “Well, I think they like the puppies. And it looks like the puppies like them too!”

My mom and the lady started talking to each other about boring grown-up stuff, like adoption paperwork.

“Mom!” I shouted.

"Sass, don't interrupt!" Mom said with one of those stern faces.

"But Mom, seriously, I found THE one!"

Mom didn't even look over at me carrying Goldie around. She kept talking to the lady as if this wasn't THE most important decision of my whole life.

Asher also found his dog—the clumsy one. He decided to name him Hamburger. He really should have asked Chloe to help him come up with a better name, but he would not listen to me about it.

Mom had packed little cages in her car for the puppies to sit in. This would keep them safe on the way home. But this made Asher burst into tears. He really wanted to hold Hamburger in his lap during the car ride.

But for once, his crying didn't bother me so much. All I knew was that being a dog mom was going to be a piece of cake.

Chapter 4

On our way home, Mom took us to the pet supply store. We got to bring in the puppies in a shopping cart since we still needed to buy some leashes. I picked pretty pink bows, a stuffed llama that squeaks, a nice warm dog bed, food, and other supplies. I picked out a pink collar and a sparkly name tag for Goldie's collar.

Everyone and their dog wanted to meet Goldie and Hamburger. They were THE cutest puppies in the whole store and probably the whole-wide world.

I knew Goldie had to have the very best toys, and I had found one she especially needed. "Momma, I just gotta have this ball thrower. It throws the ball for you, so you don't have to!"

"That looks like fun," she replied. "But maybe we should just get the puppies a tennis ball to play with. You can throw the ball for them."

"Mom. Please!"

"Sass, I said 'no,' and I mean it."

"Momma, no. They just NEED this so much! Look, it comes with batteries. Nothing comes with batteries. And it shoots it really far. Like so far. We can't throw that far, Mom. I would hurt my arm trying to throw that far. You wouldn't want me to hurt my arm, would you? Puh-leease!" Sometimes my persistence pays off. This was not one of those times, though.

"Avril . . . "

Oh no. She was using my real name. *Send help!* I thought to myself.

"I am buying you lots of great things for your dog, but I will not be buying this ball thrower. It's over one hundred dollars. End of story."

And do you know what? Asher just said, "Thank you, Mommy!" and accepted that Mom would not be buying us a ball thrower for our dogs. I did a sigh and walked along, petting Goldie and Hamburger.

Mom and Asher took Hamburger to look for supplies down another aisle. I got Miss Goldie out of the shopping cart and tried on her collar and leash to see if she would walk with me. Not long after I put her down, it happened.

Pee.

Everywhere.

It was a yellow river of pee. How does a tiny dog actually make that much pee?! To top it off, Goldie started stepping in it. And she seemed happy about it!

"Oh no! Goldie!" I exclaimed.

I tried to walk around Goldie, but now that she had peed, she was ready to play. She jumped on me and got little paw prints of pee all over my pants. It was so embarrassing!

"Hi, Sassafras!" a familiar voice called.

I looked up and saw Sally Anderson—the coolest girl in our school. And here I was, covered in pee and looking like a terrible dog mom.

"Oh, did you get a puppy?" Sally asked as she stooped down to pet Goldie.

I let out a nervous giggle. "Yeah, her name is Goldie."

Just then, Goldie jumped up on her and got pee prints all over Sally's clothes too! Sally looked down at her pants and then looked over to the puddle of pee. She looked disgusted. My face felt hot, and I just knew my face had turned bright red. I was never going to be able to go back to school again—never!

Sally suddenly waved goodbye and ran to her mom. I watched as she told her mom something. She pointed to her pants and then to Goldie. I had never been so embarrassed.

I frowned and then looked around, trying to find a way to clean up before Mom got back. I did not want to have Goldie taken away from me for being a bad dog mom! I had only just gotten her!

We walked toward the fish tanks, where I found a clean-up station with cleaning spray and towels. But Goldie was ready to go the other way, far away from the cleaning spray and towels. I tugged on her leash a little so she would follow me, but boy, was she strong. I patted my wet pant legs and tried to call her over.

By that time, Asher had walked over to show me some of the things he had picked out for Hamburger.

While I got the cleaning spray, Asher offered to help. Sometimes having a little brother is A-OK. So I asked him to get some paper towels off the roll. It turned out I should have been a little bit clearer when I said that. Before long, Asher had run around Goldie and me twice, still pulling on the paper towels. I bet he had unrolled half the roll of paper towels already! And, sure enough, Sally was watching it all. Sometimes having a little brother is not A-OK.

Finally, I just gave up and put her back in the shopping cart. I cleaned up the mess on the floor. The river of pee had become quite a big puddle. Thanks to Asher, we had plenty of paper towels.

Mom walked over just as I had finished cleaning up Goldie's mess. "Sass, what happened?"

I was so embarrassed to tell Mom that Goldie had already had an accident. Mom just smiled and led Asher and me to the bathroom so that we could wash our hands while she took care of the puppies.

The bathroom had a sink made for a giant, so I had to use all my muscles to pick up Asher so he could reach the soap. The soap dispenser was one of those machines you have to wave at just right to get it to work. This one was bonkers. It only spat out soap when our hands were nowhere near it. By the time Asher got soap, my arms felt like they were on fire. "Hurry, Asher!"

"Ah-ee! Shhhh. I trying to warsh my hands."

"You mean WASH!"

"That's what I said!"

I sighed again. I could feel my arms falling off. I was sure someone was going to have to sew my arms back on.

Mom peeked inside to check on us. "Are you guys okay in here?"

"Yep," I grunted, still trying to keep Asher up in the air.

We finally came out of the bathroom, and then we walked to the checkout counter with Mom and the puppies. Thankfully, I didn't see Sally again. But I just knew she would tell everyone at school that I got dog pee all over her. Maybe being a dog mom was not that easy after all.

Chapter 5

When we got home, Dad was there waiting for us. "Hey, kids. I heard you have some exciting news to share with me."

"We got a Hamburger!" Asher happily announced while trying to carry Hamburger into the house.

"A hamburger?!" Dad was smiling, but he was clearly confused.

"That is his puppy's name, Dad," I announced. "And this one here is Goldie."

Dad was in heaven, I think. I had never heard an adult talk with such a crazy voice. Well, besides when Aunt Violet sees Asher and starts squealing about his chubby little cheeks. Maybe Dad needed to get his own puppy.

Once Dad finally got back his normal voice, the doorbell rang. It was Chloe! And then it was a scream fest. She squealed because she was seeing the puppies for the first time. And I squealed because she was seeing them for the first time! The puppies loved Chloe almost as much as they loved Asher and me. They gave her kisses all over her face and even licked her eyeball on accident. That also made Chloe scream and laugh.

Chloe, Asher, and I took the puppies to the backyard to play. Instead, they sniffed everything. They sniffed flowers. They sniffed bricks. They sniffed the grass and the rocks and the barbecue grill. Hamburger kept sniffing a rock till it JUMPED. Then he JUMPED too!

The rock turned out to be a toad, and it didn't much care for Hamburger. Well, the toad set Goldie into a barking fit. Her bark was less than terrifying. That toad just sat there staring at her. She would not have it. She kept barking and barking. She finally had enough and swatted at it, making it jump at

Hamburger again. Poor Hamburger peed himself good!

"Holy mac and cheese!" I yelled.

Asher stood there with wide eyes. "Ah-ee, what we do?"

"Ummm. Let's move the toad out of the back-yard!"

"Not me!" Asher said.

"Asher, you know I'm afraid of frogs!"

"Ah-ee, him a toad!"

I sighed. I looked at Chloe, who shook her head and started backing away from the toad.

"Dad! Dad! Come quick! There is a TOAD. It is attacking the puppies!" I yelled. I was trying not to panic, but this was definitely an emergency if I ever saw one.

And do you know what Dad did? He just looked out the open window at the dogs and said, "They are just playing, Sass." Then he left!

It was up to me to take care of this. I closed my eyes and reached down to get the toad. By the time my hands went where the toad was, he had already hopped away. I tried again; this time, I only closed one eye. He tried to get away, but I was faster.

I stood up, smiling proudly.

Then it happened. AGAIN.

The toad peed on me!

Chloe was the first to scream, but I started crying! I couldn't just drop the toad. He could get hurt. This was a really big problem!

Asher ran toward the back patio to get away, and both puppies followed him.

"Chloe! Help!" I said, panicking.

Chloe looked around and saw one of our sandcastle buckets lying on the grass and rushed to get it. She came back and put it under my hands so that I could drop the toad inside. Squealing, she ran as fast as she could to the fence, flung open the gate, and then set the bucket down just outside the fence. She quickly slammed the gate closed.

Goldie and Hamburger bounced across the yard to the fence to make sure Chloe had gotten the job done right. Now that the toad was safely on the other side of the fence and inside a bucket, both puppies were brave again. The puppies started showing the toad who was boss . . . through the fence.

"Now what?!" Chloe said, looking terrified.

"Maybe use a stick and gently knock the bucket on its side so he can hop out," I suggested, still standing in the middle of the backyard with toad pee all over me.

Chloe did just that and then ran squealing to the back patio again.

Asher just watched and shook his head with his mouth wide open and his eyes still big. He was going to have nightmares tonight. I just knew it.

I washed my hands with a water hose while Chloe and Asher ran through the backyard, letting the puppies chase them. They even tried teaching them tricks, but the puppies were too busy rolling around in the grass and chasing butterflies and bugs. All I could think about, though, was how I had not been able to take care of the toad all by myself.

Chapter 6

After Chloe went home, it was time for Asher and me to get ready for bed. I put on my pajamas and brushed my teeth, and then I went and got the dog bed to take into my room. Of course, Mom had eyes in the back of her head and stopped me. "Sass . . . "

"Momma, Goldie will be so sad and all alone if she doesn't sleep in my room. I'm going to just put her bed on top of my bed. I'll read her a night-night story and tuck her in real good like you and Daddy do for me," I said with my sweetest voice.

"I'm sorry, Sass. That sounds really fun, but Goldie and Hamburger don't know how to go potty outside yet. I don't want them to go potty on your floor or chew up things in your room."

"But Asher gets to have Hamburger in his room!" I said, hoping that was true, so that would mean Goldie would HAVE to sleep in my room too. That would be fair.

"Both puppies are staying in the laundry room in their beds. I'm going to put down some newspaper in case they have to go potty. Speaking of pottying, have you let the puppies back inside yet?"

Oops. They'd been outside a while. When I got out there, Hamburger was chewing on a stick. And Goldie was chasing a cricket. I took them to the laundry room. Asher and I sang them songs, and I read them *Goodnight Moon*. Mom moved their food and water bowls in there too.

After that, it was Dad's turn to tuck me in and Mom's turn to tuck in Asher. I asked Dad if he thought we could visit Grandma and Paw. I wanted them to meet the puppies.

"I bet they would love that," he said.

"I don't think their chickens will like the puppies, though," I said, laughing.

"Probably not," he smiled.

As Dad tucked me into bed, he asked, "Who is your favorite? Mom or me?"

I am used to his tricks. He's a silly guy, but he cannot trick me. I am not a little kid anymore.

So I asked, "Who is your favorite? Asher or me?" I smiled at him, pleased with myself. He laughed and tickled me, and then he kissed my forehead and turned off my lights.

"I love you, Daddy."

"I love you too, Princess," he said as he closed my door.

I was nearly asleep when the puppies started hollering and howling and crying. I pulled the pillow over my head and covered my ears. Do you suppose that helped? Not one bit. I think it somehow made them louder. I wiggled under my covers and plugged my ears with my fingers. That didn't work either.

It turns out that puppy voices get louder as they

travel up laundry chutes. I sighed and tried cramming my pillow in the opening of the laundry chute. That helped! I walked back to my bed and got good and snuggled in.

I had started to doze off again when I heard a noise. It was the pillow sliding down the chute and the puppies attacking it.

I did an even bigger sigh as I got out of bed again.

I opened my door and tip-toed down the hall to Asher's room. He was sleeping like a baby brother. I could try to sneak in his bed with him, but that would be a bad idea. The last time I did that, he gave me a black eye. Little brothers roll around a lot in their sleep.

I closed his door and went back to my room. I sat on my bed a moment, trying to think of what to do. I figured that if I sang to them for a minute, they would go to sleep. I crawled down the laundry chute with my stuffed monkey, Georgie, in my hand and landed on my pillow. The puppies pounced on me with their puppy paws and puppy kisses. "Oh, you sweet puppies. You just need a songy song, huh? Don't you? Yes, you doooo."

The next thing I knew, Mom was waking me up. "Sass? What on earth? Did you sleep here all night?"

"Ugh. Where am I?" I looked around and saw I was in a dog bed and covered up with a dog blanket. Goldie and the bottom half of Hamburger were snuggled up on my pillow. Hamburger was even snoring. I rubbed my eyes and stretched. Everything hurt. *Now I know what old people feel like*, I thought. They felt like they had been sleeping in a dog bed all night.

Then, I saw it. Georgie's stuffing was hanging out of his body. I burst into tears. "Georgie!"

Mom looked over to the dog bed and let out a gasp. She knew Georgie was my favorite stuffie. I'd had him since my first birthday, and he went almost everywhere with me.

How could they do that to my poor Georgie? I was so sad, but I was also feeling really mad too. First, Goldie embarrassed me in front of Sally Anderson. Then, I got peed on by a toad. Now, this!

Hamburger must have felt guilty about eating Georgie because his little tail started wagging like crazy, and he hid his face under his dog bed.

"Well, I guess we know which dog did it, huh?" Mom shook her finger at Hamburger. "Don't you worry, Sass. It's going to be just fine. While you eat breakfast, I'll work on patching him up. He'll be good as new."

Mom wiped away my tears and sent me off to the kitchen. I was starting to have second thoughts about having puppies.

Chapter 7

I WAS GLAD IT WAS SATURDAY BECAUSE I WAS tired. I sat in the kitchen eating cereal for three Georges. It usually took one George. On top of that, it was also a rainy day. But I did have a big afternoon planned at Chloe's house watching a movie with her. We had been planning our movie day since last week.

I heard scratching and whining coming from the laundry room. I let the puppies go outside to the backyard. Then I sat back down to stare at my cereal bowl some more. I was so tired that even my freckles felt tired!

Asher bounced into the room on his bouncy ball. "Hi, Ah-ee! Where my Hamburger?"

"He's outside going potty."

Asher bounced over to the sliding glass door. "Uh-oh," he said in his cute 3-year-old voice.

I turned to look outside.

Uh-oh was right.

Our cute Goldie and Hamburger were gone. They had been replaced by mud monsters. I could not believe my eyes. Every inch of them was covered in mud, except for their excited eyes. Man, they were proud of themselves.

I grabbed my mud boots from beside the doorway and hopped around to get them on before splatting onto the hard floor.

Asher sat there on his bouncy ball and just shook his head at me. "You are getting in big trouble this time, Ah-ee. Nice knowing you."

"ME?!" I exclaimed as I pulled myself up to standing again. One of those muddy critters was HIS muddy critter.

"You done it this time. That's a big trouble for

sure." And off he bounced, quite happy I was going to get in trouble over this.

I gave up trying to get my boots on and decided I had better go barefoot. I slid open the glass door and stepped onto the patio, hoping to corral the little mud buckets. Goldie was so happy to see me that she immediately hippity-hopped all over me. Within seconds there were muddy paw prints all over my pajama pants!

And that was when I looked down to see a gigantic bug on my foot. I did a panic! I screamed and ran for my life across the patio. I was kicking my legs and flinging my foot every which way to get it off. I heard Mom coming outside to help, but I just knew that bug was going to eat my foot before she got there.

"Sass! What in the world? Why are you screaming? What is wrong?!"

"Moooommmm!" I said before squealing again. "A bug! On my foot!" Tears ran down my face.

Mom grabbed my arms to make me stop flailing

and said, "Sass, it's a drop of mud. It is not a bug!" with a laugh.

Yep, you read that right. She laughed.

Rude.

She must have seen that I was not okay and scooped me up in a hug. But that hug didn't last long because the next thing I knew, Asher was screaming.

Oh no. The dogs were in the house. Mom and I ran right into the house through the open door—the door I had left open.

As Mom and I got inside, the wet floor made us both slip and fall. Now Mom was doing a panic too!

The mud monsters were attacking the couch and the rug. Mud and paw prints were everywhere! I don't even know how they did it all so fast. Next, Goldie shook mud all over the white cabinets, and good ole Hamburger peed. I guess he was too busy rolling in the mud outside to use the potty out there. Oh, *it was bad.*

We tried catching the puppies, but we kept sliding around. Mom started to crawl after the puppies to keep from falling again. Asher just stood off to the side and watched us, occasionally shouting where the puppies were now making a mess. Goldie had gotten herself on the couch and was running back and forth while barking excitedly for Hamburger to join her. Hamburger tried to get on the couch, but his round belly kept him from hopping up there. That's when I was able to grab him.

Sensing she was next, Goldie jumped off the couch. Frantically, Mom got herself up and started sliding after Goldie.

Dad heard the fuss and came to the rescue. You see, my dad is a silly guy. He heard us screaming and thought he had better run in wearing my brother's superhero cape. I could tell even with his superhero cape on that he was surprised. His eyes got huge, and he stopped pretending real fast. Maybe he saw Mom's mad face as she was walking back into the kitchen with a very muddy Goldie in her arms. He knew it was time to be serious.

Mom, the puppies, and I all got bubble baths. Then we all scrubbed the mud off everything for about 5 or 6 Georges. That's 50 or 60 minutes in big kid talk. My scrubbing hand was as tired as my freckles.

That afternoon we all took a good nap, even the puppies. Mom also fixed Georgie, but he just didn't look quite the same with stitches.

Mom was not too upset about the door being left open since she didn't close the door either. I was upset, though. The puppies had quickly taken over everything, and they were so hard to take care of. And worse, I didn't even get to go see a movie at Chloe's house. I had been looking forward to it all week!

Chapter 8

I WORKED HARD ON MY CHORES THE WHOLE NEXT week. Asher and I did a good job keeping the puppies fed. It turned out Hamburger was a good name for Asher's puppy. Hamburger really liked to eat! He wiggled his whole body while he ate. Goldie did not like him being cute when he ate. She barked at him when he got too carried away.

Hamburger chewed up one of Asher's toys that week, and it was not able to be fixed. He cried a long time over it and went to bed crying that night. Every night that week, we went to bed early because we were so tired from taking care of the puppies. They were always getting into something they shouldn't be or making puddles on the floor.

When it was finally Friday afternoon, I got off the bus and ran straight to my house. After I ate dinner, it was time for my friends to come over to play. Chloe and her little brother came over, and so did Sophie. We had the best time playing with Goldie and Hamburger. The puppies were on their very bestest behavior and didn't have a potty accident at all.

All of us girls went up to the treehouse while Asher and Chloe's brother, Bennett, played on the little kid trampoline. We were just getting into playing Rapunzel when I heard yelping. I spotted Goldie as I came down the treehouse slide. She was playing with a tennis ball, but I didn't see Hamburger anywhere. I tried to get back to playing Rapunzel, but I kept hearing yelping.

"Asher! Hamburger is missing. I hear him crying," I shouted.

Asher and Bennett bounced to the edge of the trampoline and stuck their faces to the net that keeps them from falling off it. "I'm wookin' Ah-ee!"

Asher said. He looked hard through the net, his face smashed flat against it.

Neither of them saw Hamburger, so they kept jumping. I sighed and grumbled to myself. I was trying to have fun with my friends, and Asher was not taking care of his dog. Hearing even more yelping and howling, I decided I had better find Hamburger.

I ran around the backyard looking for Hamburger, trying to follow the sounds of his crying. I finally spotted him rolling around behind a tree with something attached to him. I ran even faster to see what had happened.

As I got closer, I realized that whatever was attached to him was alive. Hamburger had found himself a turtle. Or maybe the turtle found himself a Hamburger. There was no time to figure it out. It looked like Hamburger was going to be eaten by the turtle. It had clamped its mouth on his foot.

I looked around to see if Mom and Dad were outside. But once again, there was no one around to help.

I kneeled by Hamburger, and I said softly, "It's okay, boy. It's going to be alright." I grabbed his collar, so he could not move. With my other hand, I put a stick out next to the turtle's mouth, and it suddenly latched onto that instead!

I had done it!

Hamburger ran off, limping and crying. I followed after him as he howled. I kneeled down again and tried to pet him. Every time I put my hand near him, he backed away. His paw was hurting so bad. He licked it and then cried more. I scooted a little closer, but Hamburger let out a loud yelp as I tried to reach for him again.

I didn't want Mom and Dad to think I couldn't handle this, and I didn't want them to take our puppies away either. We couldn't even keep him from getting eaten by a turtle, the slowest animal ever! But I needed help. I ran to the back door and yelled for Mom to come quick, that Hamburger was hurt.

Mom walked quickly through the yard, and all my friends and Asher followed behind her. When

Mom saw Hamburger yelping in pain, she gasped. I couldn't stand to look at poor Hamburger because he was in so much pain, so I covered my eyes.

"Mom, is he going to be okay?" I asked.

"What happened, Sass?"

Poor Hamburger kept on crying louder and louder. And now he also had a bunch of kids looking at him. He must be SO embarrassed. I was sure that Goldie would be worried, but when I looked over my shoulder, guess what. She was STILL playing with her tennis ball like Hamburger had not almost gotten himself eaten by a turtle.

"He was over here crying, so I came to check on him." I pointed to the tree where the turtle was and said, "A turtle over there was biting him and wouldn't let go. I put a stick near its mouth, and it bit down on that instead."

Mom went to the tree where the turtle was. It no longer had that stick in its mouth. She picked up the turtle and carried it outside the fence.

Next, she picked up poor Hamburger. She used her foot to move a rock in front of the hole under our fence. That way, the turtle wouldn't be able to get back inside our yard.

"Well, it looks like Hamburger will be having his first vet appointment in the morning," Mom said as she walked Hamburger inside the house.

That was when Goldie finally stopped playing long enough to notice Hamburger was sad. She bounced along behind Mom and cried when the back door closed, and Goldie realized she couldn't follow Mom and Hamburger anymore.

Mom came back outside a few minutes later and said that Asher and I should play with our friends until it was time for them to go home, but all I could think about was sad, injured Hamburger.

Chapter 9

I READ ASHER'S FAVORITE BOOKS TO HIM TO keep him from crying so much about Hamburger being hurt. By the time I had read the fourth book, he had fallen asleep on my shoulder. Little brothers need a good big sister to take care of them sometimes.

Dad had bandaged Hamburger's leg so that he wouldn't keep licking it. Poor Hamburger whimpered a lot, but once he was asleep, I didn't hear him again.

The next morning, we all went in the car to take the puppies to their very first dogtor appointment. Get it?! Dog doctor, dogtor?! I'm hilarious.

Mom put Asher in his car seat while Dad and I

got the puppies in their crates in the back of the car. Poor Hamburger yelped a few times.

Once we got to the vet, we saw that it was a big place with lots of fun stuff for dogs. Hamburger disagreed. He shook like a leaf from the moment we walked in. He also whimpered from time to time. It didn't help that a cat in the waiting room hissed at him as we walked by.

Aside from that cat, there was a lady there with her pet ferret. Another person there had a couple of parakeets in a cage. They ruffled their feathers as we walked past, and Goldie somehow didn't seem to notice them. She was too busy smelling all the smells. We sat down next to a girl and her dog while Mom got us checked in at the front desk.

The dog next to us had beautiful long hair that was brown on her head and black and gray on her body. She was smaller than Goldie, and she wore a cute bow on her head. Goldie was not impressed. She clearly did not like me paying any attention to other dogs. Goldie huffed and set her head down on my legs, looking away from the dog beside us.

Hamburger laid in Dad's lap, still shaking and whimpering. The vet had a lot of customers, so we waited for what felt like a year—maybe two years. It was more Georges than I could count. You know time also stops when you are bored. It gave me a lot of time to think. Everything had kind of been a disaster since we brought the puppies home. I wiped tears away from my eyes and tried not to think about it, but I couldn't help it. If I were my mom and dad, I wouldn't let me keep the puppies. I put my head down on the small table beside my chair so that no one could see me cry.

Eventually, a lady with pink hair came in and called out, "Hamburger?" When we got up, she said, "I'm Carrie, and I'll be taking care of Hamburger today."

"I love your hair!" I gave her a little smile.

Carrie said, "Aw, well, thank you. Let me guess. This puppy with the bandage is Hamburger?"

Asher was amazed. "HOW did you know that?!"

She laughed and then looked at her notes. "It looks like Hamburger has an ouchie," she said before she took us over to some scales in the next room. I got to help Goldie get weighed, even though she didn't need to see the vet today. It was a huge chore because she was SO wiggly! Carrie weighed Hamburger since he couldn't stand up on all four legs very well.

Next, Carrie took Hamburger's temperature and listened to his belly.

"What's that?" Asher asked. He pointed to the listening thing that Carrie was using.

"This is a stethoscope. It helps me hear Hamburger's heart and lungs. It also lets me listen to his belly to make sure it's making lots of good noises in there."

Asher and I both got to listen too. That made me want to be a veterinarian. I could be a veterinarian and a paleontologist and a doctor and an artist. All those.

Next, Carrie asked lots of questions about what the puppies do all day. I told her, "They just pee and eat and get me in trouble a lot." The mud mishap was still on my mind.

She unwrapped Hamburger's foot and then looked at it. She tried to bend it, but he yelped. Tears filled my eyes again as I wondered if Hamburger would be okay.

Carrie patted my shoulder, and then she left and came back with a man in a white coat. He said his name was Dr. Boatsman. I thought that was kind of a weird name for a vet. Maybe he should have been a boat captain instead. Or maybe he was like me and liked to be lots of things. Maybe he was a boat captain AND a vet. I liked him already.

We introduced him to Hamburger and Goldie. Dr. Boatsman asked me if Goldie's last name was "Locks." I looked at him like he was crazy. Who would name their dog Goldie . . . Locks?

Ohhhhhhhh. I get it! I giggled and shook my head. What a silly guy!

First, he listened to Hamburger's heart and belly, and then he checked all over Hamburger's body. He frowned as he looked at Hamburger's foot.

"Carrie, can you take Hamburger to get an X-ray, please?"

I watched as Miss Carrie took Hamburger to a back room. "What's an X-ray?" I asked.

"That's where we take a picture with a special machine that can see Hamburger's bones. We check the picture for any broken bones or injuries," the vet said.

A broken bone sounded scary and painful—poor Hamburger.

Dr. Boatsman talked to Asher and me about how to take care of our puppies. Most of this stuff we already knew because we are smarties. He gave me a list of foods that dogs cannot eat, like onions, grapes, chocolate, and garlic! I felt bad they couldn't have grapes or chocolate, but they won't be missing much if they never eat onions and garlic. Yuck!

When Carrie got back with the X-ray, Dr. Boatsman looked at it carefully on a light-up board. "Well," he said. "It looks like nothing is broken. Since everything looks good, little Hamburger likely just has a bruise and is going to want to take it easy for a while. We can send him home with some medicine for his pain." He wrapped up Hamburger's leg and gave Dad some supplies so that he could change the leg wrap at home.

Finally, Carrie put a big cone around Hamburger's head to keep him from trying to lick and bite at his hurt foot. It was the funniest sight! Hamburger looked sad and mad and embarrassed. And the cone was so big that he was just worn out. He did a plop on the floor and just laid there until we picked him up to go home.

Chapter 10

ONCE WE GOT HOME FROM THE VET, I MADE Hamburger a comfy bed. The doctor had bandaged his leg with light blue wrapping tape. I took one of my markers and drew lots of hearts on it so that Hamburger would know I loved him.

That week was hard. Taking care of the puppies was exhausting. Plus, they also had gotten me into a lot of trouble, and I wasn't able to go to Chloe's house for a movie. At least Sally didn't tell everyone at the school about the dog pee.

But as I sat looking at poor, sad Hamburger I was just so happy he would be okay.

That afternoon, Chloe and Bennett got to come to play at our house again. We pretended to be ninjas for a long time, but the boys decided they wanted to go outside to play by themselves.

Chloe and I decided we would do a science experiment with food coloring, milk, and dish soap. Chloe had seen it on a TV show. Mom helped us pour the milk onto a dinner plate, but Chloe and I did the rest. We put lots of drops of colored dye right in the middle of the plate. When we put a drop of soap on the dye, the colors ran far away from it. They spread out into a big rainbow of colors. It was super cool!

Even though my bestie was over at my house, I still made sure to take the puppies out to go potty. I also carried Hamburger over to his food and water bowl to eat and drink. I took his cone off for just a minute.

Hamburger was a bit more chipper. He followed Goldie around the yard smelling all the same things they smelled the day before. I guess they needed to make sure none of the smells got away since the last time they smelled those smells. Sometimes poor

Hamburger would run into things wearing his cone, so that kept us laughing.

Hamburger was worn out, so I put him back inside the house to rest. Chloe and I stayed outside and worked a long time with Goldie. And guess what! We taught her to sit!

Even Chloe was impressed. "Wow! She learned to sit so fast. She has got to be the smartest puppy in the whole world!"

This made me feel super proud to be Goldie's dog mom.

Once we came back inside, Goldie sniffed Hamburger to make sure he didn't have any fun while she was outside. When Chloe and Bennett had to go home for dinner, Asher and I sat down on the couch to watch some TV.

We had only been sitting there a little while when Dad walked in and asked us to follow him for a family meeting. Asher and I followed him to his office, and Mom was there too. I gulped as I sat down. I just knew this was going to be bad.

He said, "Sass, when your mom and I first talked about getting you a puppy, we were not sure you were ready."

Oh, no. I knew it! I thought to myself.

"But every day, you do your chores, and you take great care of Goldie. You even help your brother take care of Hamburger. But last night, you did something even more special. You heard Hamburger was in trouble, and you did all the right things to get help for him. And ever since, you have made sure he has been well taken care of."

As Dad finished, he handed me an award. It was a certificate that he had printed on bright pink paper. It said, "This award is presented to Sassafras," and below that, it said really big: "BEST DOG MOM."

This was not what I expected at all! I smiled so big that I was pretty sure I was glowing. I was a dog mom! And I was a good one!

Asher exclaimed, "You win, Ah-ee!"

I laughed and hugged Asher. Then, I gave Mom and Dad a big hug. I ran to show Goldie and Hamburger my award before hanging it up on the refrigerator. I read it one more time: BEST DOG MOM. I couldn't help but smile. This was something to be really proud of!

That night, I drew lots of pictures in my journal about all our adventures. I drew pictures of muddy dogs, a toad, a turtle eating Hamburger, and even Hamburger in his cone. The last picture I drew was of me hugging Goldie with a big smile on both of our faces. Yes, the puppies were a lot of work and got me into some trouble, but they were also a lot of fun. It was okay that we made mistakes. I was still learning, just like the puppies were. And I wouldn't trade them for anything.

This
AWARD
is presented to
Sassafras
BEST
DOG
MOM

THE END

About the Author
Janet R. Adams

Janet R. Adams writes books for children and young adults. Her goal is to inspire young readers in the hopes they will become life-long readers. She lives in the United States with her husband, children, and dogs. Stay connected with Janet at janetradams.com.

Leave a Review

Thank you for supporting an independent author. If you enjoyed this book, please help spread the word and consider submitting an honest review of this book.

Lightning Source UK Ltd.
Milton Keynes UK
UKHW041828170521
383897UK00001B/104

9 781953 499059